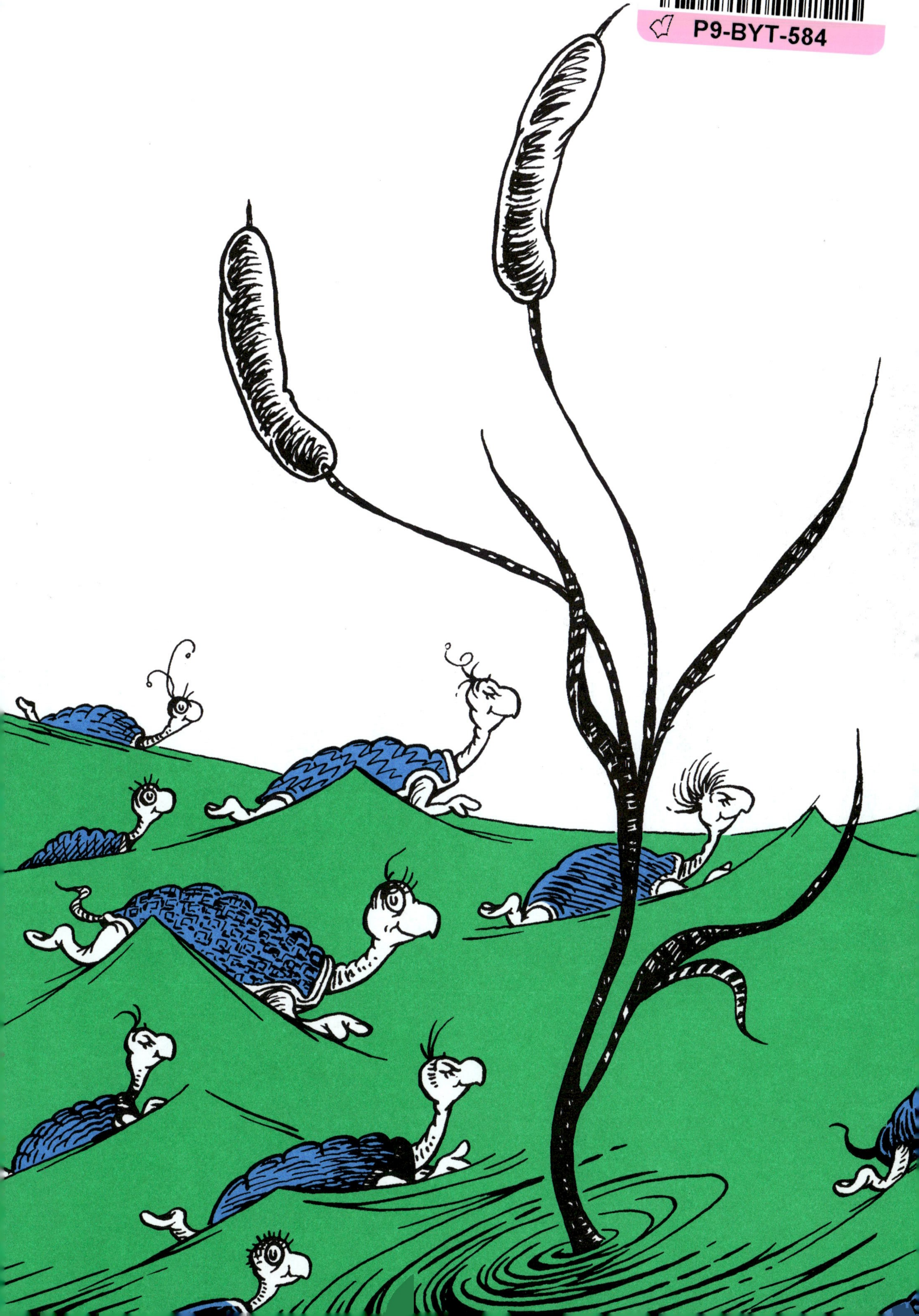

Yertle the Turtle and Other Stories

YERTLE the TURTLE and Other Stories

By Dr. Seuss

RANDOM HOUSE · NEW YORK

Published in the United States by Random House Children's Books, a division of Random House, Inc., New York.
Originally published by Random House Children's Books, a division of Random House, Inc., New York, in 1958.

Random House and colophon are registered trademarks of Random House, Inc.

Visit us on the Web!
www.randomhouse.com/kids
www.seussville.com

Educators and librarians, for a variety of teaching tools, visit us at www.randomhouse.com/teachers

This title was originally cataloged by the Library of Congress as follows:
Geisel, Theodor Seuss,   1904   Yertle the turtle, and other stories,   by Dr. Seuss [pseud.]
New York, Random House   [1958]   unpaged.   illus.   29cm.
I. Title.   PZ8.3G276Ye   58-9011
ISBN: 978-0-394-80087-5 (trade) ; 978-0-394-90087-2 (lib. bdg.)

Printed in the United States of America   105

Random House Children's Books supports the First Amendment and celebrates the right to read.

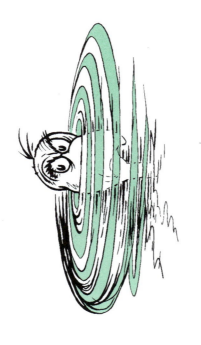

This Book is for

The Bartletts of Norwich, Vt.

and for

The Sagmasters of Cincinnati, Ohio

YERTLE the TURTLE

On the far-away Island of Sala-ma-Sond,
Yertle the Turtle was king of the pond.
A nice little pond. It was clean. It was neat.
The water was warm. There was plenty to eat.
The turtles had everything turtles might need.
And they were all happy. Quite happy indeed.

They *were* . . . until Yertle, the king of them all,
Decided the kingdom he ruled was too small.
"I'm ruler," said Yertle, "of all that I see.
But I don't see *enough*. That's the trouble with me.
With this stone for a throne, I look down on my pond
But I cannot look down on the places beyond.
This throne that I sit on is too, too low down.
It ought to be *higher!*" he said with a frown.
"If I could sit high, how much greater I'd be!
What a king! I'd be ruler of all I could see!"

So Yertle, the Turtle King, lifted his hand

And Yertle, the Turtle King, gave a command.

He ordered nine turtles to swim to his stone

And, using these turtles, he built a *new* throne.

He made each turtle stand on another one's back

And he piled them all up in a nine-turtle stack.

And then Yertle climbed up. He sat down on the pile.

What a wonderful view! He could see 'most a mile!

"All mine!" Yertle cried. "Oh, the things I now rule!
I'm king of a cow! And I'm king of a mule!
I'm king of a house! And, what's more, beyond that,
I'm king of a blueberry bush and a cat!
I'm Yertle the Turtle! Oh, marvelous me!
For I am the ruler of all that I see!"

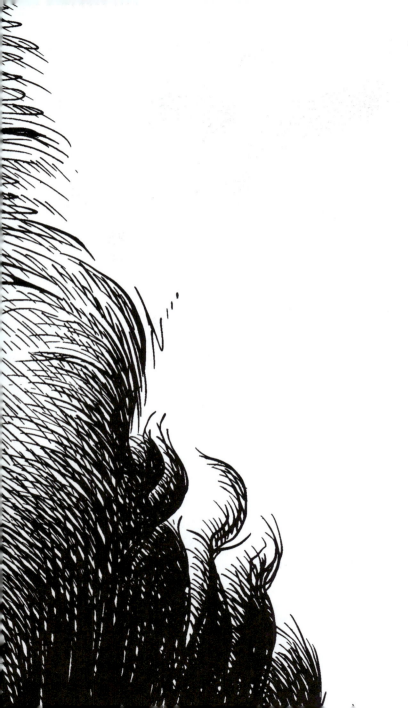

And all through that morning, he sat there up high
Saying over and over, "A great king am I!"
Until 'long about noon. Then he heard a faint sigh.
"What's *that*?" snapped the king
And he looked down the stack.
And he saw, at the bottom, a turtle named Mack.
Just a part of his throne. And this plain little turtle
Looked up and he said, "Beg your pardon, King Yertle.
I've pains in my back and my shoulders and knees.
How long must we stand here, Your Majesty, please?"

"SILENCE!" the King of the Turtles barked back.
"I'm king, and you're only a turtle named Mack."

"You stay in your place while I sit here and rule.
I'm king of a cow! And I'm king of a mule!
I'm king of a house! And a bush! And a cat!
But that isn't all. I'll do better than *that*!
My throne shall be *bigher*!" his royal voice thundered,
"So pile up more turtles! I want 'bout two hundred!"

"Turtles! More turtles!" he bellowed and brayed.

And the turtles 'way down in the pond were afraid.

They trembled. They shook. But they came. They obeyed.

From all over the pond, they came swimming by dozens.

Whole families of turtles, with uncles and cousins.

And all of them stepped on the head of poor Mack.

One after another, they climbed up the stack.

THEN Yertle the Turtle was perched up so high,
He could see forty miles from his throne in the sky!
"Hooray!" shouted Yertle. "I'm king of the sky!
I'm king of the birds! And I'm king of the trees!
I'm king of the butterflies! King of the bees!
Ah, me! What a throne! What a wonderful chair!
I'm Yertle the Turtle! Oh, marvelous me!
For I am the ruler of all that I see!"

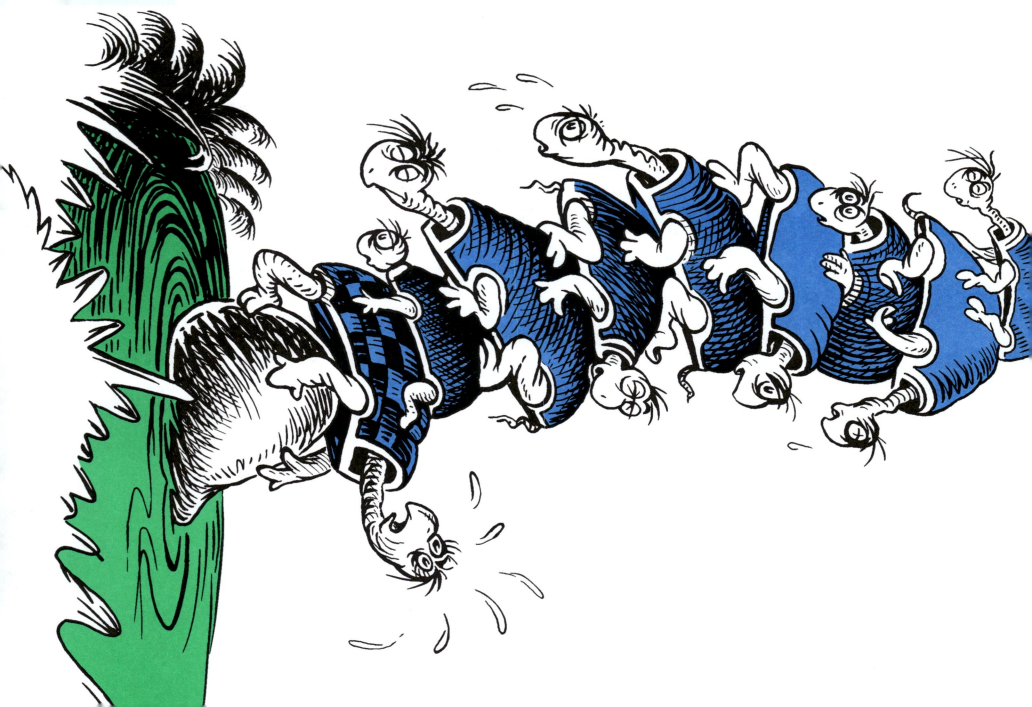

Then again, from below, in the great heavy stack,
Came a groan from that plain little turtle named Mack.
"Your Majesty, please . . . I don't like to complain,
But down here below, we are feeling great pain.
I know, up on top you are seeing great sights,
But down at the bottom we, too, should have rights.
We turtles can't stand it. Our shells will all crack!
Besides, we need food. We are starving!" groaned Mack.

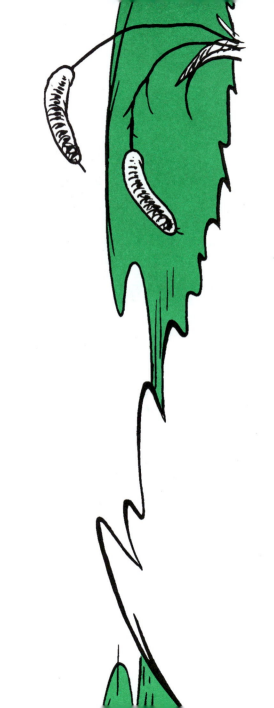

"You hush up your mouth!" howled the mighty King Yertle.

"You've no right to talk to the world's highest turtle.

I rule from the clouds! Over land! Over sea!

There's nothing, no, NOTHING, that's higher than me!"

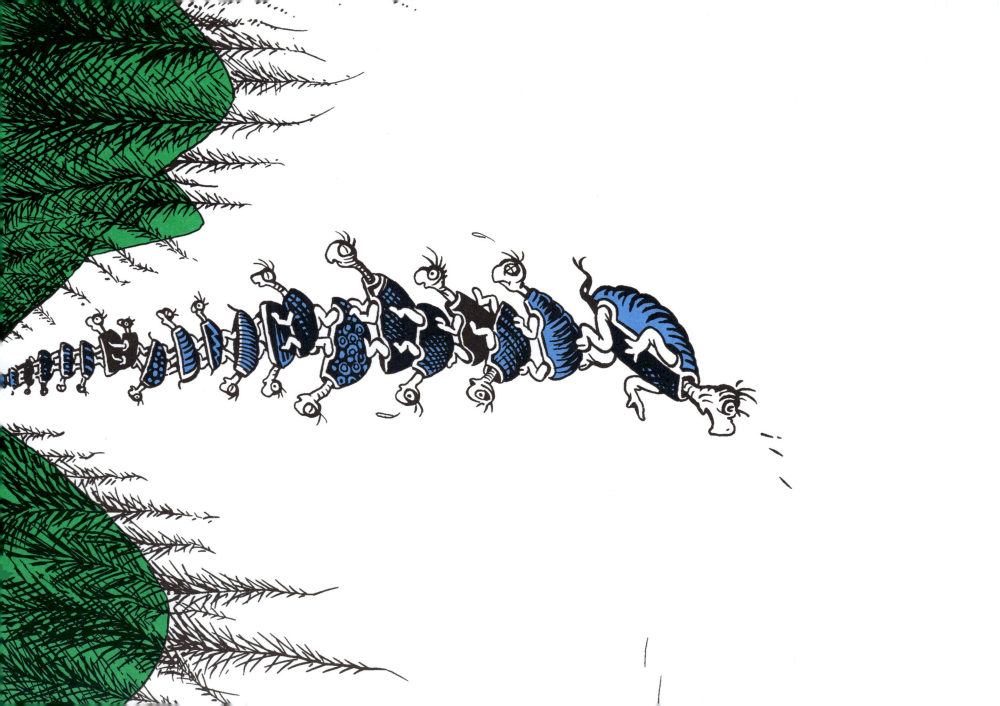

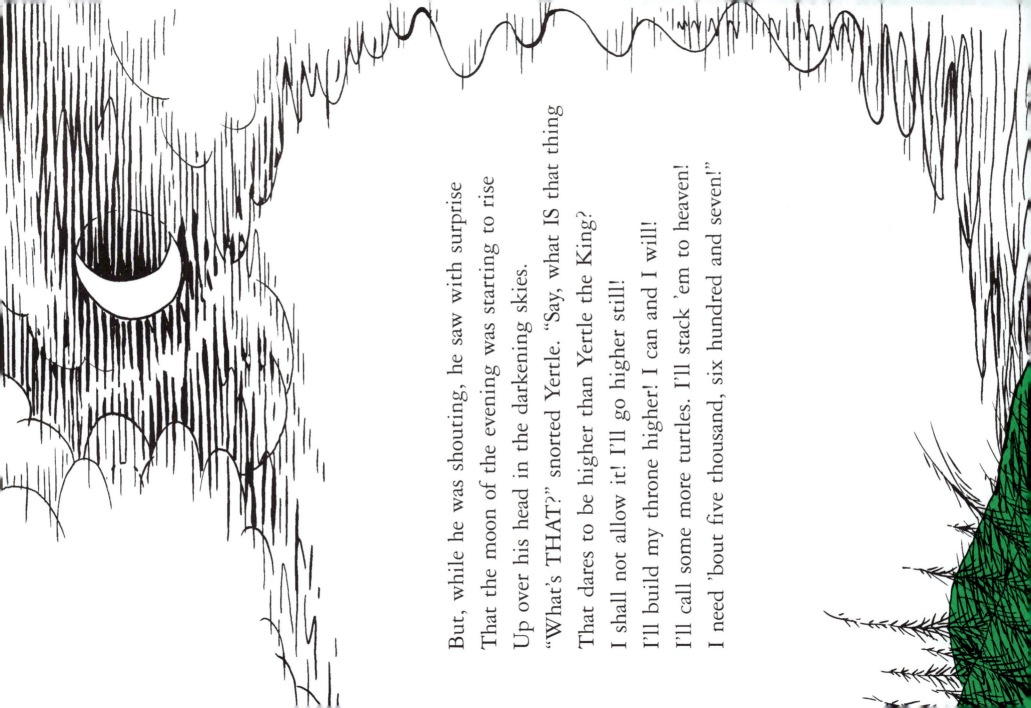

But, while he was shouting, he saw with surprise
That the moon of the evening was starting to rise
Up over his head in the darkening skies.
"What's THAT?" snorted Yertle. "Say, what IS that thing
That dares to be higher than Yertle the King?
I shall not allow it! I'll go higher still!
I'll build my throne higher! I can and I will!
I'll call some more turtles. I'll stack 'em to heaven!
I need 'bout five thousand, six hundred and seven!"

BURP!

But, as Yertle, the Turtle King, lifted his hand
And started to order and give the command,
That plain little turtle below in the stack,
That plain little turtle whose name was just Mack,
Decided he'd taken enough. And he had.
And that plain little lad got a little bit mad
And that plain little Mack did a plain little thing.
He burped!
And his burp shook the throne of the king!

And Yertle the Turtle, the king of the trees,
The king of the air and the birds and the bees,
The king of a house and a cow and a mule . . . .
Well, *that* was the end of the Turtle King's rule!
For Yertle, the King of all Sala-ma-Sond,
Fell off his high throne and fell *Plunk!* in the pond!

And today the great Yertle, that Marvelous he,
Is King of the Mud. That is all he can see.
And the turtles, of course . . . all the turtles are free
As turtles and, maybe, all creatures should be.

GERTRUDE McFUZZ

There once was a girl-bird named Gertrude McFuzz
And she had the smallest plain tail ever was.
One droopy-droop feather. That's all that she had.
And, oh! That one feather made Gertrude so sad.

For there was another young bird that she knew,
A fancy young birdie named Lolla-Lee-Lou,
And instead of *one* feather behind, she had *two*!
Poor Gertrude! Whenever she happened to spy
Miss Lolla-Lee-Lou flying by in the sky,
She got very jealous. She frowned. And she pouted.
Then, one day she got awfully mad and she shouted:
"This just isn't fair! I have *one*! She has *two*!
I MUST have a tail just like Lolla-Lee-Lou!"

So she flew to her uncle, a doctor named Dake
Whose office was high in a tree by the lake
And she cried, "Uncle Doctor! Oh, please do you know
Of some kind of a pill that will make my tail grow?"

"Tut tut!" said the doctor. "Such talk! How absurd!
Your tail is just right for your kind of a bird."

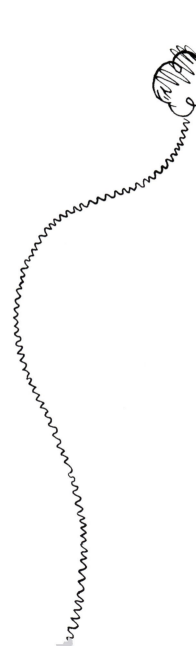

Then Gertrude had tantrums. She raised such a din

That finally her uncle, the doctor, gave in

And he told her just where she could find such a pill

On a pill-berry vine on the top of the hill.

"Oh, thank you!" chirped Gertrude McFuzz, and she flew

Right straight to the hill where the pill-berry grew.

Yes! There was the vine! And as soon as she saw it
She plucked off a berry. She started to gnaw it.
It tasted just awful. Almost made her sick.
But she wanted that tail, so she swallowed it quick.
Then she felt something happen! She felt a small twitch
As if she'd been tapped, down behind, by a switch
And Gertrude looked 'round. And she cheered! It was true!
Two feathers! Exactly like Lolla-Lee-Lou!

Then she got an idea! "Now I know what I'll do . . . .
I'll grow a tail *better* than Lolla-Lee-Lou!"

"These pills that grow feathers are working just fine!"
So she nibbled *another* one off of the vine!

She felt a *new* twitch. And then Gertrude yelled, "WHEE!
Miss Lolla has only just *two*! I have *three*!
When Lolla-Lee-Lou sees this beautiful stuff,
She'll fall right down flat on her face, sure enough,
I'll show HER who's pretty! I certainly will!
Why, I'll make my tail even prettier still!"

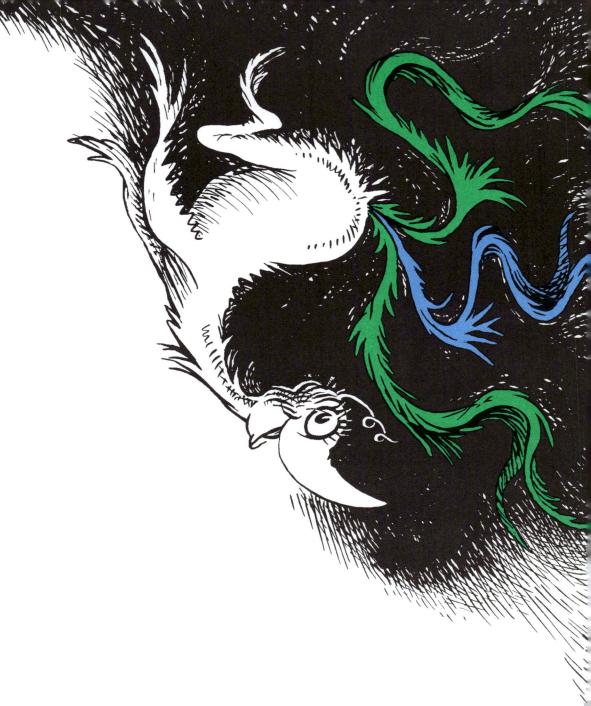

She snatched at those berries that grew on that vine.
She gobbled down four, five, six, seven, eight, nine!
And she didn't stop eating, young Gertrude McFuzz,
Till she'd eaten three dozen! That's all that there was.

Then the feathers popped out! With a *zang*! With a *zing*!
They blossomed like flowers that bloom in the spring.
All fit for a queen! What a sight to behold!
They sparkled like diamonds and gumdrops and gold!
Like silk! Like spaghetti! Like satin! Like lace!
They burst out like rockets all over the place!
They waved in the air and they swished in the breeze!
And some were as long as the branches of trees.
And *still* they kept growing! They popped and they popped
Until, 'long about sundown when, finally, they stopped.

"And NOW," giggled Gertrude, "The next thing to do
Is to fly right straight home and show Lolla-Lee-Lou!
And when Lolla sees *these*, why her face will get red
And she'll let out a scream and she'll fall right down dead!"

Then she spread out her wings to take off from the ground,
But, with all of those feathers, she weighed ninety pound!
She yanked and she pulled and she let out a squawk,
But that bird couldn't fly! Couldn't run! Couldn't walk!

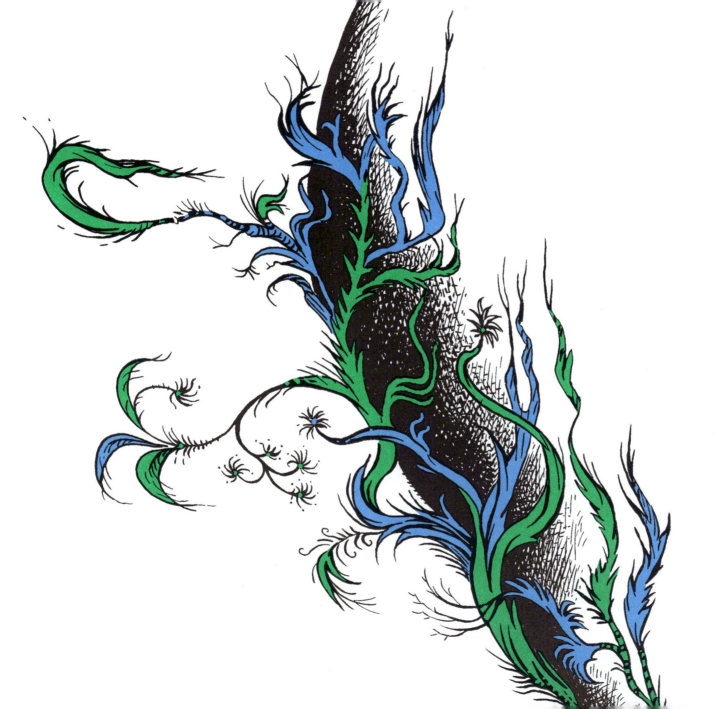

And all through that night, she was stuck on that hill,
And Gertrude McFuzz might be stuck up there still
If her good Uncle Dake hadn't heard the girl yelp.
He rushed to her rescue and brought along help.

To lift Gertrude up almost broke all their beaks
And to fly her back home, it took almost two weeks.
And *then* it took almost another week more
To pull out those feathers. My! Gertrude was sore!

And, finally, when all of the pulling was done,
Gertrude, behind her, again had just one . . .
That one little feather she had as a starter.
But now that's enough, because now she is smarter.

The BIG BRAG

The rabbit felt mighty important that day
On top of the hill in the sun where he lay.
He felt SO important up there on that hill
That he started in bragging, as animals will
And he boasted out loud, as he threw out his chest,
"Of all of the beasts in the world, I'm the best!
On land, and on sea . . . even up in the sky
No animal lives who is better than I!"

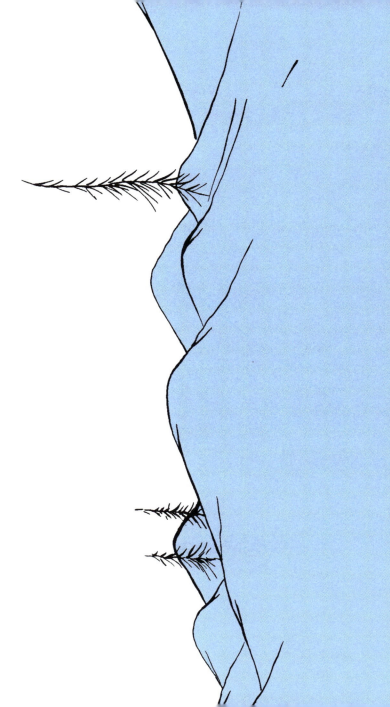

"What's *that?*" growled a voice that was terribly gruff.

"Now why do you say such ridiculous stuff?"

The rabbit looked down and he saw a big bear.

"*I'm* the best of the beasts," said the bear. "And so there!"

"You're not!" snapped the rabbit. "I'm better than you!"

"Pooh!" the bear snorted. "Again I say Pooh!

You talk mighty big, Mr. Rabbit. That's true.

But how can you prove it? Just what can you DO?"

"Hmmmm . . ." thought the rabbit,

"Now what CAN I do . . . ?"

He thought and he thought. Then he finally said,

"Mr. Bear, do you see these two ears on my head?

My ears are so keen and so sharp and so fine

No ears in the world can hear further than mine!"

"Humpf!" the bear grunted. He looked at each ear.

"You *say* they are good," said the bear with a sneer,

"But how do *I* know just how far they can hear?"

"I'll prove," said the rabbit, "my ears are the best.

You sit there and watch me. I'll prove it by test."

Then he stiffened his ears till they both stood up high

And pointed straight up at the blue of the sky.

He stretched his ears open as wide as he could.

"*Shhh!* I am listening!" he said as he stood.

He listened so hard that he started to sweat

And the fur on his ears and his forehead got wet.

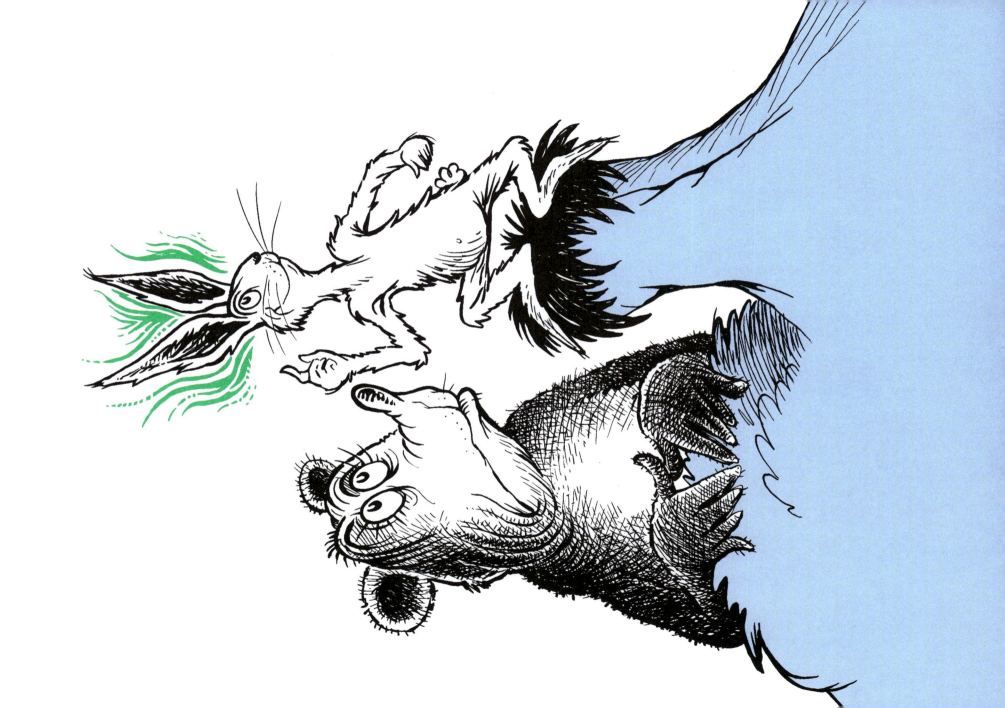

For seven long minutes he stood. Then he stirred
And he said to the bear, "Do you know what I heard?
Do you see that far mountain . . . ? It's ninety miles off.
There's a fly on that mountain. I just heard him cough!
Now the cough of a fly, sir, is quite hard to hear
When he's ninety miles off. But I heard it quite clear.
So you see," bragged the rabbit, "it's perfectly true
That my ears are the best, so I'm better than you!"

The bear, for a moment, just sulked as he sat

For he knew that *his* ears couldn't hear things like *that*.

"This rabbit," he thought, "made a fool out of me.

Now *I've* got to prove that I'm better than he."

So he said to the rabbit, "You hear pretty well.

You can hear ninety miles. *But how far can you smell?*

I'm the greatest of smellers," he bragged. "See my nose?

This nose on my face is the finest that grows.

My nose can smell *anything*, both far and near.

With my nose I can smell twice as far as you hear!"

"You can't!" snapped the rabbit.

"I can!" growled the bear

And he stuck his big nose 'way up high in the air.

He wiggled that nose and he sniffed and he snuffed.

He waggled that nose and he whiffed and he whuffed.

For more than ten minutes he snaff and he snuff.

Then he said to the rabbit, "I've smelled far enough."

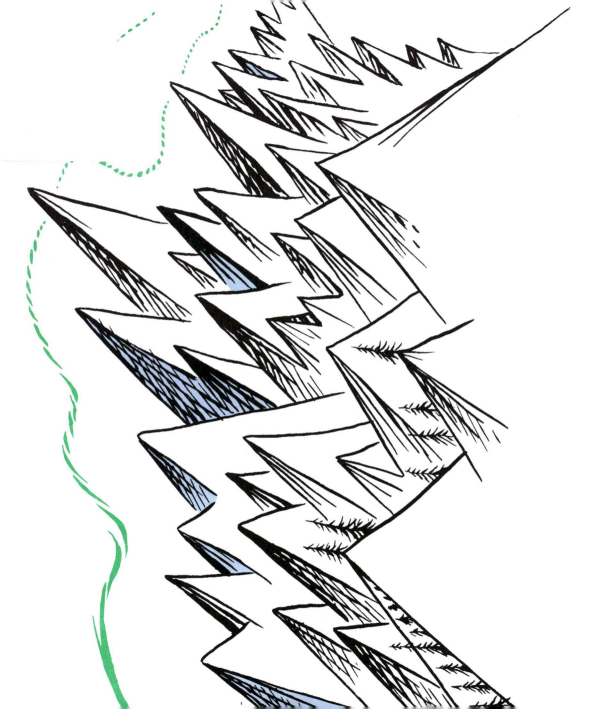

"All right," said the rabbit. "Come on now and tell
Exactly how far is the smell that you smell?"

"Oh, I'm smelling a *very* far smell," said the bear.
"Away past that fly on that mountain out there.
I'm smelling past many great mountains beyond
Six hundred miles more to the edge of a pond."

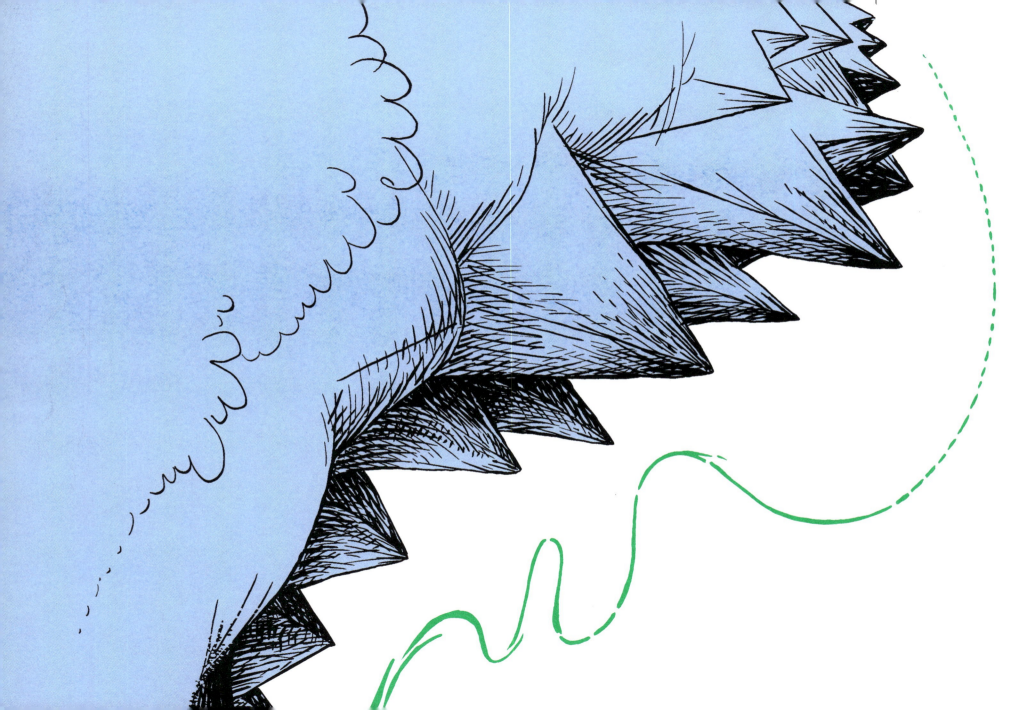

"And 'way, 'way out there, by the pond you can't see,
Is a very small farm. On the farm is a tree.
On the tree is a branch. On the branch is a nest,
A very small nest where two tiny eggs rest.
Two hummingbird eggs! Only half an inch long!
But my nose," said the bear, "is so wonderfully strong,
My nose is so good that I smelled without fail
That the egg on the left is a little bit stale!
And *that* is a thing that no rabbit can do.
So you see," the bear boasted, "I'm better than you!
My smeller's so keen that it just can't be beat . . ."

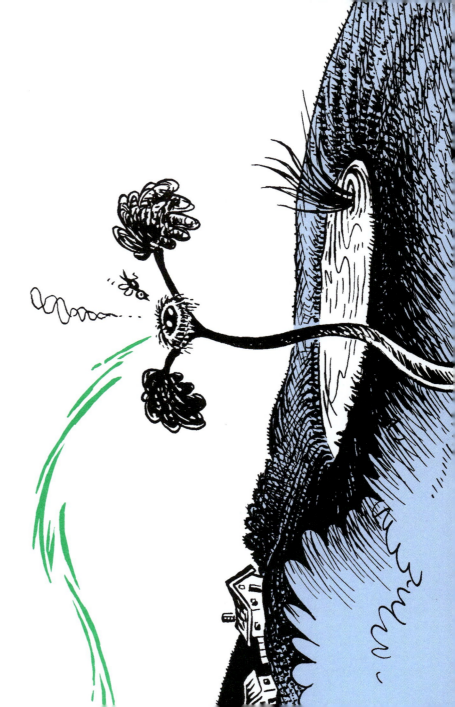

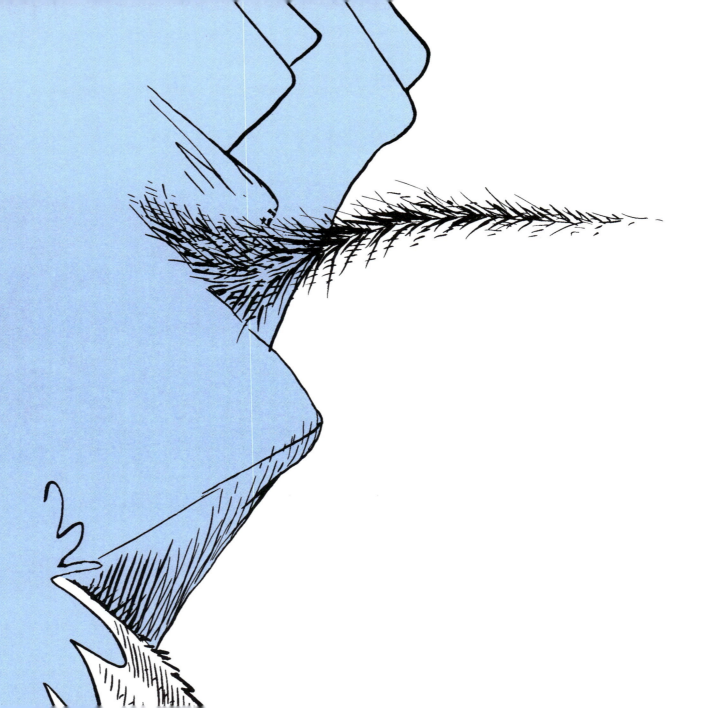

"What's that?" called a voice
From 'way down by his feet.
The bear and the rabbit looked down at the sound,
And they saw an old worm crawling out of the ground.

"Now, boys," said the worm, "you've been bragging a lot.
You both think you're great. But *I* think you are not.
You're not half as good as a fellow like me.
You hear and you smell. *But how far can you SEE?*
Now, *I'm* here to prove to you big boasting guys
That your nose and your ears aren't as good as my eyes!"

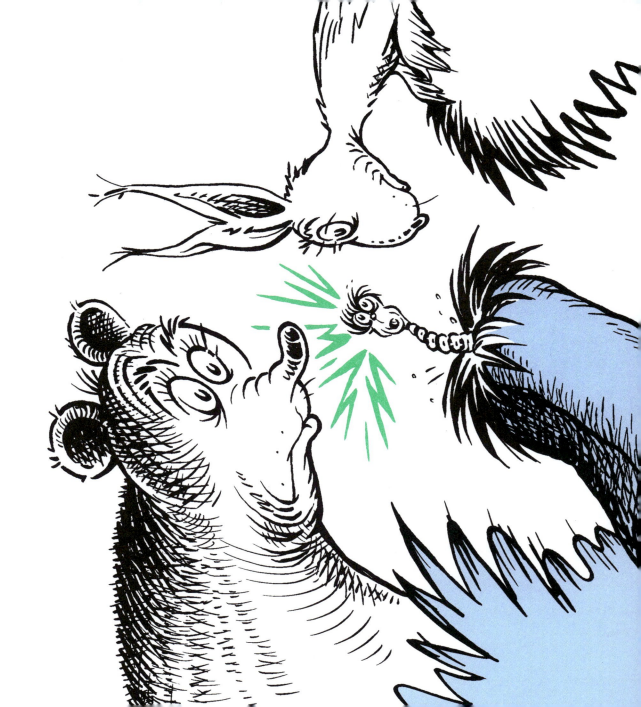

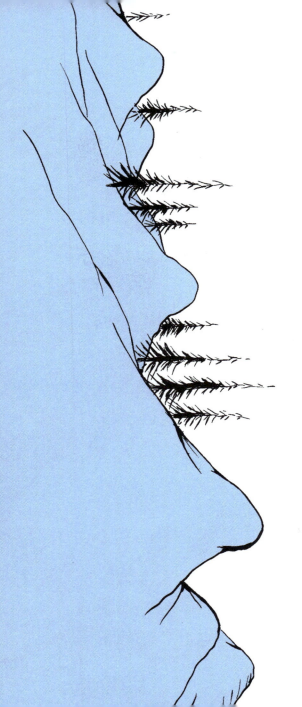

And the little old worm cocked his head to one side
And he opened his eyes and he opened them wide.
And they looked far away with a strange sort of stare.
As if they were burning two holes in the air.
The eyes of that worm almost popped from his head.
He stared half an hour till his eyelids got red.
"That's enough!" growled the bear.
"Tell the rabbit and me
How far did you look and just what did you see?"

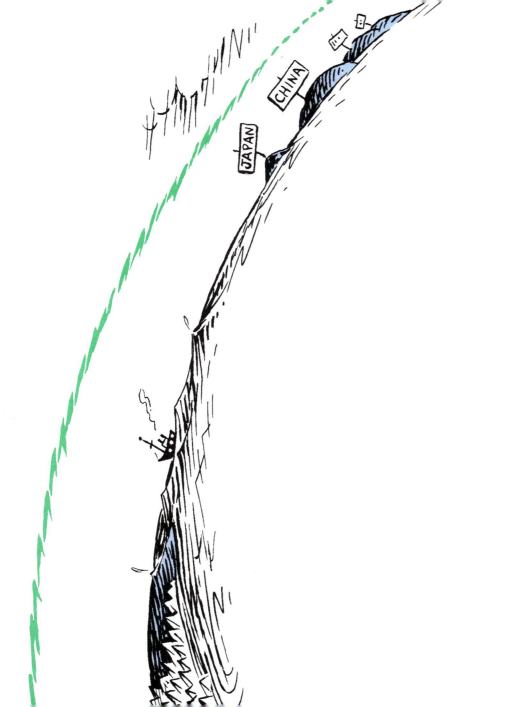

"Well, boys," the worm answered, "that look that I took
Was a look that looked farther than *you'll* ever look!
I looked 'cross the ocean, 'way out to Japan.
For I can see farther than anyone can.
There's no one on earth who has eyesight that's finer.
I looked past Japan. Then I looked across China.
I looked across Egypt; then took a quick glance
Across the two countries of Holland and France.
Then I looked across England and, also, Brazil.
But I didn't stop there. I looked much farther still.

"And I kept right on looking and looking until

I'd looked 'round the world and right back to this hill!

And I saw on this hill, since my eyesight's so keen,

The two biggest fools that have ever been seen!

And the fools that I saw were none other than you,

Who seem to have nothing else better to do

Than sit here and argue who's better than who!"

Then the little old worm gave his head a small jerk
And he dived in his hole and went back to his work.

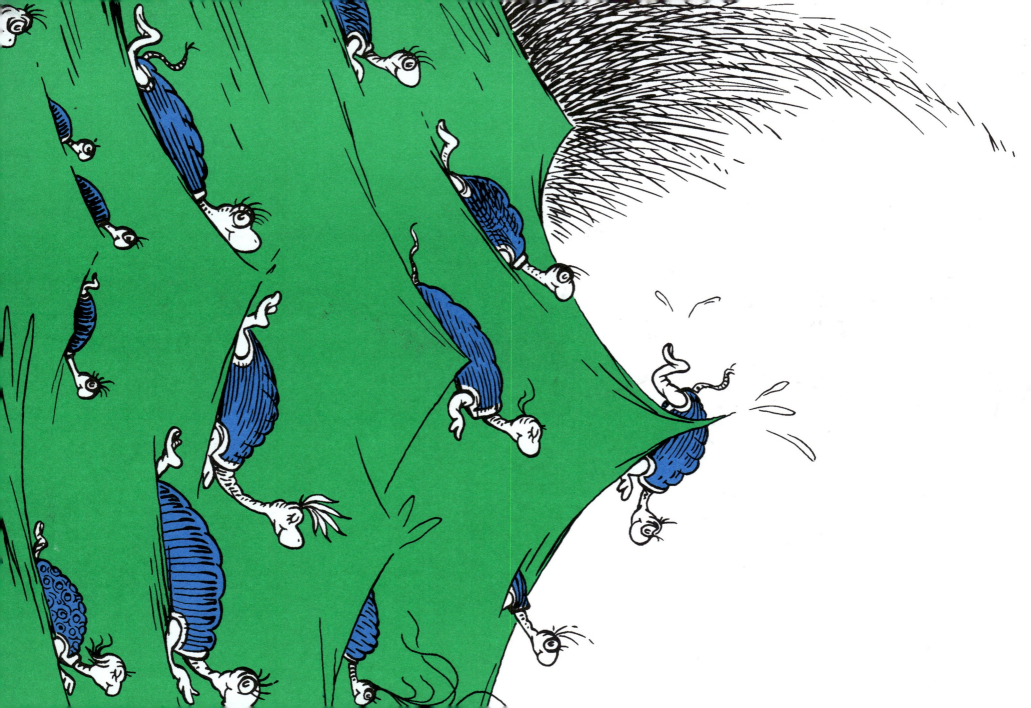